I0589017

Marriage is Murder

Nick Hall

A Samuel French Acting Edition

SAMUEL FRENCH

FOUNDED 1830

SAMUELFRENCH.COM
SAMUELFRENCH-LONDON.CO.UK

FOR PRODUCTION ENQUIRIES

UNITED STATES AND CANADA
Info@SamuelFrench.com
1-866-598-8449

UNITED KINGDOM AND EUROPE
Plays@SamuelFrench-London.co.uk
020-7255-4302

Each title is subject to availability from Samuel French, depending upon country of performance. Please be aware that *MARRIAGE IS MURDER* may not be licensed by Samuel French in your territory. Professional and amateur producers should contact the nearest Samuel French office or licensing partner to verify availability.

MUSIC USE NOTE

Licensees are solely responsible for obtaining formal written permission from copyright owners to use copyrighted music in the performance of this play and are strongly cautioned to do so. If no such permission is obtained by the licensee, then the licensee must use only original music that the licensee owns and controls. Licensees are solely responsible and liable for all music clearances and shall indemnify the copyright owners of the play(s) and their licensing agent, Samuel French, against any costs, expenses, losses and liabilities arising from the use of music by licensees. Please contact the appropriate music licensing authority in your territory for the rights to any incidental music.

IMPORTANT BILLING AND CREDIT REQUIREMENTS

If you have obtained performance rights to this title, please refer to your licensing agreement for important billing and credit requirements.

CHARACTERS

Paul Butler
Polly Butler

SETTING

Paul Butler's Upper West Side studio apartment,
New York

ACT ONE

Scene 1: Thursday evening
Scene 2: Later that evening
Scene 3: Friday morning

ACT TWO

Scene 4: Friday evening
Scene 5: Later that evening
Scene 6: Saturday morning

iv

ACT I

Scene 1

The setting is the single room of Paul Butler's Manhattan apartment, in an older building. The entrance is in a raised alcove, Stage Right. Flanking the entrance in the side walls of the alcove are two doors; Upstage to a closet, Downstage to the bathroom. In the rear, Upstage, wall of the room, a swinging door to the kitchen. In the shorter Left wall a window. About Center is a sofa-bed. In front of it a large chest used as a coffee table. Behind the couch a Parsons table with a lamp, a phone, and an answering machine. The phone is not cordless. The cord to the phone is long. There is a stool or hassock against the Rear wall. A straightback chair extreme DR. Under the window DL a large round table serving as desk and cluttered. Beside it a comfortable, rolling, swivel desk chair. A sideboard against the Rear wall. Bookshelves. Basically the room is gracious, but now it is unbelievably untidy and cluttered. There is one seating area on the couch that is free and clear. Everywhere else are clothes both clean and dirty, newspapers, magazines, books, typescript, bottles, coffee mugs, shoes, bathrobes, towels, a pizza box, etc., etc. Not only is every surface cluttered, but also parts of the floor. There is an unbound pile of manuscript Down Center. However, the basic impression is of mess, not filth.

*A KNOCKING at the door. Repeated. Sound of KEY in
door. POLLY enters. SHE is an attractive woman
wearing a crisply fashionable outfit. SHE heaves in a
large suitcase, a briefcase, a handbag and a small
paper shopping bag. SHE dumps the suitcase and
briefcase as soon as SHE is in. Calling out and
switching on LIGHTS.*

POLLY. Paul? Paul, are you here? It's me.

*(Realizing he isn't, SHE looks around the apartment. Puts
down handbag and paper bag. Puts suitcase and
briefcase in closet which is cluttered. Opens paper bag,
takes out dagger. Tests point of dagger gingerly with
fingertip. Crosses to Parsons table. Carefully puts point
of dagger on table and presses handle, blade
disappears into handle. Repeat. Now confident, presses
point against palm of hand, blade into handle. Finally,
stabs herself. Pleased, puts knife down on the table and
notices the light on the answering machine. Presses
button.*

SANDRA—*voice on machine:* "Paul? Paul, this is Sandra.
Where are you? When does the Wicked Witch of the
West arrive? Give me a call about tonight. Okay."

*Tape ends. POLLY punches machine off and resets it.
Takes compact out of handbag, checks appearance,
crosses to bathroom, fumbling in bag. Exits bathroom,
closing door.*

*PAUL enters. HE is attractive and the same age as Polly.
Probably wearing a tweed jacket and chinos, HE is
slightly rumpled. HE carries a bag with a bottle in it
from the liquor store. Crosses to sideboard and puts*

down bottle—gin, tosses flattened paper bag onto a pile of stuff on the floor. Taking off jacket, crosses to sofa, sits. Reaches behind himself and turns on answering machine.

SANDRA— "Paul? Paul, this is Sandra. Where are you? When does the Wicked Witch of the West arrive? Give me a call about tonight. Okay."

PAUL switches tape off, picks up phone and dials.)

PAUL. (*On phone.*) Hi, listen, about tonight ... It's me, Paul. I guess this evening's off. Probably just as well, I couldn't really afford it ... In a couple of hours. She said she'd call as soon as she got in ... I dunno, the Plaza, the Pierre, somewhere expensive ... I've no idea, she didn't say ... Sandra, I do not know why my ex-wife, the big Hollywood screenwriter wants to see little me ... That's not it. She does not want to stay ... No, I don't want her to stay either ... Listen, I haven't seen her in eighteen months, since the divorce ...

(POLLY enters from the bathroom, unseen by PAUL. Listens.)

PAUL. ... Yes, I'm sure ... Sandra, I've told you before: not as attractive ... not as nice ... not as young ... Well, she is pretty bright ... Yes, I do, it's just yours is a different kind of bright. It's more, um, more—I sort of think of you as physically intelligent ...

(POLLY has and crossed to behind him, picking up the knife. SHE taps him on the shoulder. HE gives a huge cry: "Whaaat!" and leaps up holding the phone.)

PAUL. (*To Polly.*) Polly! Polly! You nearly gave me a heart attack. (*On phone.*) It's Polly. She's here. (*To Polly.*) This is Sandra. (*On phone.*) Sandra, Polly, my ex-wife. (*To Polly.*) Polly, Sandra my ... er, typist. We were just saying ... I was just saying ... Did you hear what I was saying?

(*POLLY raises the knife for him to see. On phone.*)

PAUL. I think she heard what we were saying ... She's got a knife that's why I think that. She's only kidding. (*To Polly.*) Aren't you kidding?

(*SHE stabs him, driving the knife into the torso. SHE holds it there a second. On phone.*)

PAUL. She's not kidding. Aaah!

(*HE drops the phone and clutches his stomach as POLLY "withdraws" the knife. HE sinks down into sitting on the sofa. POLLY picks up the dangling phone.*)

POLLY. (*On phone.*) Hello, Sandra?... The Wicked Witch of the West has arrived! (*Hangs up.*)
PAUL. (*Still startled.*) Polly! Polly! Oh, my God, Polly, what have you done?
POLLY. Gotcha! That's what I've done, gotcha. You're dead, Paul. You should lie down. Dead people do that. Face down, I think. Face down looks better on the cover of a book. (*Showing him, SHE presses the point of the knife so the blade retracts, a couple of times.*) Gotcha, gotcha, gotcha.

PAUL. I think I'm having a heart attack.
POLLY. No, you're not.
PAUL. I am, I'm having a heart attack.
POLLY. Nonsense.

(Right behind Paul's head the PHONE rings. PAUL reacts "Aaah!" POLLY gets phone.)

POLLY. *(On phone.)* Hello ... Who?... I'm sorry Gummy Bear can't talk right now, he's having a heart attack.

PAUL. *(Snatches phone. On phone.)* Hello and help ... Yes, I'm alive ... No, I'm not okay ... Yes, that was her ... I'll tell you what she's doing here ... *(To Polly.)* What are you doing here?

POLLY. I've come for the ruby slippers.

PAUL. *(On phone.)* She's come for the ruby ... Listen, I'll call you later. 'Bye. *(Hangs up. Gasping.)*

POLLY. You couldn't find an adult, Gummy Bear? *(Looking around. Scathing.)* I'd forgotten how the other half lives.

PAUL. Just what do you think you are doing?

POLLY. I'm doing what we always did. Acting out our books, getting the details correct. Rehearsing writing a murder. We always acted it out.

PAUL. You're not supposed to be here 'till later.

POLLY. Guess who took an earlier flight.

PAUL. Well, you'll never get away with it.

POLLY. *(Pulling off latex gloves.)* Of course, I will. Please notice the gloves—no fingerprints.

PAUL. If I were dead, the police would catch you just like that. *(Finger snap.)* They always suspect the spouse.

POLLY. Ex-spouse. And this ex-spouse could prove she was in California at the time.

PAUL. You're right here and they'd check the airlines.

POLLY. I travelled under an assumed name, wearing a slight disguise, having paid a travel agent in cash.

PAUL. They'd check to see if you were in California tonight.

POLLY. I am. Nobody knows I'm here, except Ellen and she's on my side. If this were real life I'd have an alibi. Someone would give me an alibi.

PAUL. In a murder case—name one.

POLLY. Jimmy Tyrrell.

PAUL. Jimmy Tyrrell! You must be out of your mind. No one would believe Jimmy Tyrrell. He's a crook.

POLLY. He's our agent.

PAUL. I rest my case.

POLLY. He's helped me a lot recently. And he'd give me an alibi.

PAUL. Why? There'd have to be something in it for him. What's his percentage?

POLLY. Well, it would mean I had just committed the perfect murder. The kind of intriguing, fascinating case that leaves the police baffled and can only be solved by ...

PAUL. Please don't say it.

POLLY. ... by Miss Charlotte Hayakawa. Jimmy thinks there's a market for more Charlotte Hayakawa mysteries.

PAUL. We wrote three Miss Charlie formula murder mysteries, none of which exactly set the world on fire.

POLLY. People read them, like them. They made it from hardcover to paperback. They're still selling. Not big, but still in print and still selling. Jimmy says that's the key.

PAUL. To what?

POLLY. Money. I assume you'd like more money. Jimmy says there have been inquiries about Miss Charlotte Hayakawa from a large—Jimmy emphasized large—production company. They're talking movies that would be TV here and theatrical overseas. Each based on a novel. It's a total marketing concept, beyond Jessica Fletcher.

PAUL. Why Miss Charlie? I mean, there are more famous detectives.

POLLY. They've all been adapted: Sam Spade, Hercule Poirot, Marlowe, Whimsey, Sherlock, Miss Marple—they've all been done. They're not virgins anymore.

PAUL. Bite your tongue! Miss Marple is so a virgin. And quite possibly Sherlock.

POLLY. Virgins to the screen. They want a fresh figure like Miss Charlotte Hayakawa. Also Jimmy says the publishing company's affiliated production company's transnational holding company's parent company is Japanese. And they love mysteries.

PAUL. Ah so! It's the inscrutability, I guess.

POLLY. So Miss Charlotte Hayakawa caught their eye.

PAUL. She's not even Japanese. Do they know how we got her name? Do they know that we looked at the mailboxes downstairs and chose Charlotte from 729, 'cos that seemed right, but her last name was Brown, which didn't, so we picked another last name.

POLLY. Thank God, we picked Hayakawa.

PAUL. I picked Hayakawa. You, of course, picked that Italian jock Fellepelle, which was far too ethnic.

POLLY. (*Incredulous.*) You think Hayakawa isn't ethnic?

PAUL. It's a whole different thing.

POLLY. Which we never explained.

PAUL. Maybe she's divorced. Married and divorced.

POLLY. Why would she be divorced?

PAUL. Because she was impossible to live with. Gives her a touch of real, ugly life.

POLLY. Speaking of real life, as I came up in the elevator, there was a Japanese man—obviously Hayakawa—and a woman and as he got off, he said: "Goodnight, Charlotte."

PAUL. There you see, life imitates pulp.

POLLY. Our mysteries were not pulp.

PAUL. They certainly weren't *Anna Karenina.*

POLLY. I don't want to write *Anna Karenina;* I can't even spell *Anna Karenina.* As a matter of fact, I've always thought Anna Karenina was pushed! A crowded train station, one shove, under the engine she goes. I'm sure it was murder. Men were always getting away with murder in those days. Look at Emma Bovary. I mean, if you accept *that* suicide, I've got a bridge to sell you.

PAUL. I'm beginning to see where Miss Charlie gets her suspicious little mind.

POLLY. She's a fictional detective; of course, she's suspicious.

PAUL. And rude and bossy.

POLLY. She is not rude and bossy.

PAUL. Oh, yes she is. She's always bursting in unannounced and disturbing everybody. That's rude. And I know where she gets it.

POLLY. Where?

PAUL. You. She gets it from you.

POLLY. Well, Jimmy Tyrrell and I both think she's sort of nice. She's smart, she's educated, reasonably literate, observant, perceptive, sensitive and humorous and she got it from me. She also has street smarts.

PAUL. She got that from me.

POLLY. You have no street smarts—none. Remember that thunderstorm when you bought the umbrella on the street?

PAUL. That umbrella was a bargain!

POLLY. Paul, it wasn't waterproof. She got street smarts from me.

PAUL. She always knows better than anybody else. And tells them.

POLLY. (*Starts to move papers.*) And she's neat and tidy. But I don't think she got that from you. You could safely dispose of a body in here. They'd never find it.

PAUL. Don't tempt me. (*HE rushes to take papers and puts them back.*) She's always poking about in other people's things. She can't leave anything alone. She got that from you.

POLLY. (*Moving away.*) She likes to sit down occasionally. She got that from me too. Why don't you clean this place up?

PAUL. And she nags. She nags people.

POLLY. She does not nag.

PAUL. Face it, she's a pain in the ass.

POLLY. She is not a pain in the ass.

PAUL. Oh, yes, you are.

POLLY. Hold it! I thought we were talking about Charlie.

PAUL. *Miss* Charlie. She's single. Understandably single.

POLLY. Well, she didn't get that from me, did she?

PAUL. She would've done, if I'd known then what I

know now. I want a divorce.

POLLY. We've got a divorce.

PAUL. Well, it's obviously not working. You're still here. Why are you here?

POLLY. I'm here so we can get together again.

PAUL. Couldn't live without me, hunh?

POLLY. As writers. (*Beat.*) I want us to write another Miss Charlie mystery.

PAUL. No.

POLLY. Why not?

PAUL. Because of the people you have to work with.

POLLY. The only person you'd have to work with is me.

PAUL. Exactly. Well, do it yourself. Apparently she got it all from you.

POLLY. I didn't mean that, Paul. She got lots of wonderful things from you. And if you give me a minute, I'll think of one.

PAUL. Please, take your time.

POLLY. Let me see ...

PAUL. No rush, I can put on some music. How about the entire Ring Cycle?

POLLY. There you are: music! She likes Julie Andrews records. She could only have got that from you. Or, of course, Julie Andrews.

PAUL. That's it? My entire contribution to this team was "The Lonely Goatherd"?

POLLY. Okay, okay, so you were the one during our very first murder who bought the axe and cut up the body and took it to New Jersey.

PAUL. That's when you gave up eating red meat.

POLLY. I, of course, had to stay behind and clean up

the mess you made. Blood everywhere. I told you to use the bathroom.

PAUL. It was full of pantyhose and Woolite.

POLLY. I also told you to use a store mannequin, but no, you had to be authentic and buy a side of beef, which we couldn't afford.

PAUL. I'd planned on eating it when we were through.

POLLY. Paul, nobody wants to eat something that's been buried for days.

PAUL. I was gonna dig it right up.

POLLY. Then you should've marked the grave.

PAUL. You don't mark shallow graves in New Jersey.

POLLY. After that we settled for a gentler, kinder murder.

PAUL. We used a lot of blunt instruments. The good thing about blunt instruments is there's generally one around and you don't have to do much research.

POLLY. Those were the days. That's when we invented Miss Charlie.

PAUL. We didn't really invent Miss Charlie. We sort of stole a bit and borrowed a bit and put her together. Like Frankenstein.

POLLY. Well, she's ours now, for better or worse.

PAUL. Or she was until about eighteen months ago when you went west.

POLLY. Best move I ever made.

PAUL. If you can sell a story idea over lunch in less words than it takes to order the food. I can't.

POLLY. I can. And now that I live in California we could set a mystery there. I know the background. How about *Miss Charlie Goes Hollywood*. Let's say she goes to visit a friend or relative who, it's gonna turn out, is the victim.

PAUL. A surprise visit—she bursts in?

POLLY. Yes. And they're dead on arrival—her arrival. Would you buy that?

PAUL. In a heartbeat.

POLLY. She's sort of touring around, and she drives cross-country. And she arrives at the house in her bright yellow 1965 Mustang.

PAUL. (*Exploding.*) She got that from me!

POLLY. Well, now that it's mine she got it from me.

PAUL. I can't believe you did that.

POLLY. Paul, you got the rent-stabilized apartment and the Julie Andrews records—I got the car.

PAUL. It's not fair.

POLLY. I was leaving; you were staying. Of course, it was fair.

PAUL. I loved that car.

POLLY. I know.

PAUL. I mean, I really loved that car more than anything.

POLLY. I know.

PAUL. It was perfect. Perfect. I cherished that car. An American classic in flawless condition.

POLLY. I guess I didn't tell you about the left front fender.

PAUL. What?

POLLY. Miss Charlie didn't see the Budweiser truck.

PAUL. Miss Charlie is a bitch and guess where she got it.

POLLY. She got it in the left front fender just outside Fresno.

PAUL. (*Seething.*) There's something you should

understand about me and Miss Charlie. I don't like her. I never liked her. Never. I always knew it wouldn't last. And, by God, I was right. She went west first chance she got, and when she went west she went in a wonderful car she wasn't entitled to and proved she was a half-assed driver. And she got that from you, damn you.

POLLY. (*Strong.*) She exists! She's published. She's hard working, she doesn't sit around whining, and she gets the job done. She got that from me too. (*Deliberately.*) If it were up to you, she'd still be an idea late at night over drinks.

PAUL. (*Mutters.*) I need a drink.

POLLY. (*Continuing on.*) She needed a push and I pushed.

PAUL. Incessantly.

POLLY. You just liked being a writer. You hated actually writing. Take a good look at yourself, Paul; you're pushing middle-age with no pension and a bad back. And one last thing about Miss Charlie—unlike you, she can generate enough money to fix the left front fender.

PAUL. What?

POLLY. She can make money—serious money. In which case, as far as I'm concerned, you can have the wretched car. It's a thirty-year-old Ford and I want an automatic transmission.

PAUL. (*Beat.*) When do we start?

POLLY. Gotcha.

PAUL. Can we do this?

POLLY. Of course, we can do it. We used to be good at this.

PAUL. Yeah, well, we used to be young and in love too, but that doesn't mean we still are, does it?

POLLY. We can do this. We need to make a commitment to the mysteries. The Japanese need a guarantee of at least four more in three years before they'll go to contract.

PAUL. Tell me, why come back to get me involved in this? If there's so much money in Miss Charlie, why aren't you going ahead and doing it by yourself?

POLLY. I can't.

PAUL. *(Very smug.)* Aha! You need me.

POLLY. No. I don't. Legally, I have to have you. She's copyrighted in both our names. I don't get her 'till you're dead. Or, conversely, you get her when I'm dead.

PAUL. What happens when we're both dead?

POLLY. As I recall, if we both get hit by a bus, we left her to Jimmy Tyrrell.

PAUL. So if I die, you get this character who's suddenly worth a lot of Japanese money?

POLLY. Yup.

PAUL. Now there's a motive for murder. You could have used a real knife.

POLLY. The thought crossed my mind.

PAUL. *(Thoughtfully.)* And, of course, because of your alibi, you're not even really here.

POLLY. Don't get any ideas, Paul. I'm here and we've got to get to work.

PAUL. What about your screenplays? Rumor has it your scripting a vast science-fiction epic?

POLLY. That's a one shot. I can do two things at once. This will lead to a whole series of screenplays. Megabucks.

PAUL. I'll drink to that. Martini? Miss Charlie loves martinis.

POLLY. And she got it from you.

PAUL. (*Picking up bottle.*) Lucky, I took the last money I had in the world and bought gin, isn't it?

POLLY. Did you get vermouth?

PAUL. (*Crossing to kitchen.*) Vermouth is eternal—I have the first vermouth I ever bought. Won't take a minute. (*Surprisingly hospitable.*) Have a seat. (*Exits kitchen.*)

POLLY. (*Alone. Dry.*) Thank you very much. (*Considers the room.*) I'd sit on the floor, but I don't think there's room.

(*Clears another seat on the sofa by piling stuff on the chest. Sits. Considers, clears an area on the chest by piling stuff on the floor. Sits. PAUL enters with two martinis—no olives. HE comes and sets down drinks on the chest.*)

PAUL. Here we are then. Two writers. Two martinis. Sounds professional to me.

POLLY. Enjoy it. It's the last you're having for a while. (*Raising glass.*) Miss Charlie Goes Hollywood.

PAUL. (*Scathing.*) Yes, well, we'll work on that title tomorrow. These look naked. I'm out of olives. I can't afford olives.

POLLY. Miss Charlie always has olives.

PAUL. She's independently wealthy.

POLLY. She didn't get that from us.

PAUL. I think that's creative writing. How about a twist?

(*SHE sits her drink down again, as HE crosses to kitchen. Both drinks on chest.*)

PAUL. I mean we are writing a murder mystery. I think there's a lemon somewhere. (*Exits kitchen.*)

POLLY. (*Looks at drinks a second. Considers.*) Yes, Paul, you're right. A twist is just what we need. (*Carefully and deliberately switches glasses. Sits back.*)

PAUL. (*Re-enters with two slivers of lemon peel. As HE twists and drops lemon.*) I'm going along with this, but I want it clearly understood it's business, purely business.

POLLY. Purely business.

PAUL. I am only writing this because I need the money.

POLLY. You feel like a prostitute?

PAUL. Certainly not. Prostitutes get cash every night and their agents call them.

POLLY. We used to rehearse everything, try it out, make sure it worked, surprise each other.

PAUL. I loved it.

POLLY. So did I. We'll need a plot—you're good at that. Clues, false leads, red herrings. And a neat solution, of course. Not like real life.

PAUL. We don't deal with real life. Never have.

POLLY. (*Raising glass.*) The game's afoot.

PAUL. (*With glass.*) You wanted murder. You got murder. From here on out it's murder all the way.

(*THEY drink deeply. POLLY would scream, but SHE can't breathe, SHE clutches her throat, gasping and sputtering, HER face contorted.*)

PAUL. Gotcha!

CURTAIN

Scene 2

(The same. Later. PAUL is standing with the phone, pretending to talk on it. POLLY is attempting to strangle him with a stocking or pantyhose. SHE has climbed onto the back or arm of the sofa in order to reach. The stocking is around his hand and the phone as well as his neck. It is not working.)

PAUL. *(On phone, pretending.)* ... so I will certainly tell you if anything suspicious happens, Miss Charlie ... Yes, I will be careful ... No, I won't let anyone sneak up behind me ... And just one other thing I think I ought to mention, Miss Charlie, someone is trying to strangle me.

POLLY. *(Breaks off business. Exasperated.)* Now you've ruined the surprise. You're not supposed to notice me.

PAUL. How could I possibly not notice you?

POLLY. Paul, sit down.

PAUL. Why, do you have bad news?

POLLY. I can't reach, if you're standing up. And I can't get the thing around your neck anyway. Don't you ever change hands or ears or something? We're going to have to think of something else.

PAUL. *(On phone.)* Hello, Miss Charlie, we'll have to get back to you on this murder. *(Hangs up.)* In books and movies people are always getting strangled while they're on the phone.

POLLY. Well, obviously, somebody didn't do their

research thoroughly. I'm surprised anyone ever gets murdered, if it's this hard. Okay, we need some ideas here. Not on the phone and not standing up. It would help if he were kneeling down.

PAUL. Why? Is he religious?

POLLY. Maybe looking for something—that would help. (*Idea.*) I've got it. (*Artificially.*) Darling, would you get me that thing we keep in the chest.

PAUL. What thing?

POLLY. The thing we keep in the chest.

PAUL. What thing? What chest?

POLLY. (*Strained.*) Anything, just so we keep it in *that* chest, darling.

PAUL. (*Overdoing it.*) Oh, I get it. (*Opens chest.*) I'll get you the thing from the chest, shall I?

POLLY. (*Mutters.*) I wonder if all murderers have this problem with their victims.

PAUL. (*Reaches in chest and casually hands her from the top a couple of items of dirty laundry.*) Here you are, darling. Just what you've been looking for—the thing from the chest.

POLLY. What is this?

PAUL. Well, let me see—that's a sock, and this is a tee-shirt ...

POLLY. This is your dirty laundry. That's disgusting.

PAUL. You gotta keep that stuff somewhere.

POLLY. (*Tossing it aside.*) Not that thing. The other thing.

PAUL. (*Snapping.*) The other thing? What other thing?

POLLY. The thing we keep at the bottom of the chest *under* all the stuff.

PAUL. Oh, that. Well, why didn't you say the thing

under all the stuff?

POLLY. I didn't think I'd have to. The thing you have to get on your knees to find. That thing, for heaven's sake.

PAUL. (*Getting on knees.*) Oh, the have-to-get-on-your-knees-into-the-chest-under-the stuff-all-the-way-at-the-bottom-head-down-so-you-can-sneakup-behind-me-thing. Right? (*HE is into chest.*)

POLLY. (*Hisses.*) Right!

PAUL. I'm looking. (*HE is largely obscured by the lid which opens toward audience. Tosses out some socks.*)

POLLY. About damn time.

PAUL. I need to go to the laundry more often. I'm not enjoying this.

POLLY. (*Throwing pantyhose over his head and starting to strangle.*) Funny, I am. I've got you now. Maybe I should put my knee in your back. Just for leverage, you understand. There, like that. Paul, stop fumbling down there. You're supposed to be dying. Okay, let's go: eyes popping, tongue protruding, starting to turn blue—now we're cooking. This is great, and she can hide the body in the chest. One final pull—and it's over. (*Lets go. Moves away.*) That's it. Gotcha. Paul, that's it. That'll work. What d'you think, Paul, what d'you think? (*Moves back.*) Paul, you have just been murdered; you can get up now.

PAUL. (*Gets up. HE has pulled on the pantyhose as a mask and lofts a huge axe. Igor accent.*) Maybe he isn't dead.

(*POLLY screams.*)

PAUL. All alone, little girl?

POLLY. Oh, my God.

PAUL. Scream away, my pretty.

POLLY. Paul, stop it. This is not our kind of murder; we don't do hatchet jobs; we do kinder, gentler murders.

(PAUL—Igor laugh.)

POLLY. Just stop it. Right now. Put that down and take it off.

(PAUL does so.)

POLLY. What are you doing with a huge, great axe in the middle of Manhattan?

PAUL. I got it to cut up that huge, great side of beef, remember. And I gotcha with it.

POLLY. Very funny. Now get rid of it. Be careful, Paul. I have just drunk a large poisoned martini. You could've killed me.

PAUL. Cyanide kills you; that was citrate of magnesium; citrate of magnesium just ... just ...

POLLY. Miss Charlie does not use bathroom humor, Paul. Now who are the most likely murderers?

PAUL. Husbands and wives.

POLLY. *(Straightening things in a desultory fashion. Holds up black bra SHE has found.)* Because?

PAUL. They're husbands and wives. *(Snatching bra.)* Of course, not all husbands and wives commit murder. Some of them just walk out. That happens.

POLLY. We don't write that kind of book.

PAUL. *(Beat.)* I do. I am.

POLLY. *(Wary.)* Oh, really, what's it about?

PAUL. Us. You and me.

POLLY. What's it called?

PAUL. *A Deadly Coherence.* It's a post-modern vaudeville of a politically-incorrect deconstructed contemporary marriage.

(POLLY stares. Beat.)

PAUL. I thought I'd take a shot at real life.

POLLY. Big mistake, Paul. You don't know anything about real life. In fact, with the chest there, how do you open the sofa-bed? *(Starts to seriously tidy room.)*

PAUL. Most of the time, I don't really bother. I use it as is—longways.

POLLY. Sandra must be very agile.

PAUL. We generally go over there.

POLLY. Wise decision.

PAUL. *(Deliberately.)* But as a matter of fact, she *is* quite agile.

POLLY. Murder. We must think of a murder.

PAUL. I have one in mind.

POLLY. Me too. Now let's think of one for a book. I'd really like an unusual murder, lots of atmospherics and a bizarre weapon like the famous frozen leg of lamb. I also like crossbows and curare. Oh, and poisoned chocolates. I love poisoned chocolates.

PAUL. You think you're up to date and you're trapped in the thirties.

POLLY. Okay, what's your favorite weapon?

PAUL. An out-of-order sign.

POLLY. What?

PAUL. An out-of-order sign. The victim has a heart

condition. The murderer puts an out-of-order sign on the elevator door. Victim climbs stairs—heart attack—dies. Simple, elegant, flawless.

POLLY. What if he doesn't die?

PAUL. No harm done. That's why it's flawless. It's Agatha Christie, of course.

POLLY. Well, we can't steal that from Agatha. I mean, we could, but not that obviously. Better stick with strangling. And we'll need a motive. Why would you want to strangle anyone?

PAUL. 'Cos she took a mint condition '65 Mustang and smashed the left front fender.

POLLY. (*Picks up some clothes.*) That's not a motive for murder.

PAUL. Sure it is.

POLLY. (*Finds bundle heavy.*) What have you got in here? (*Takes pistol out of it.*) What is this? This really looks real.

PAUL. (*Sharply.*) It is real! Don't touch it! Put it down!

POLLY. What are you doing with a real gun?

PAUL. (*Taking it from her.*) I'm keeping it for Tommy Fellepelle.

POLLY. What is he? Mafia?

PAUL. No, he'd just like to be. He's away with his family and he didn't want to leave it in an empty apartment. (*Will put it down on table DL.*)

POLLY. You know, Paul, in a murder mystery neatness counts. While I'm staying here, we're going to have to get this place organized, tidy it up.

PAUL. Repeat that.

POLLY. We're going to have to get this place ...

PAUL. (*Interrupting.*) No, not the tidy part. The staying here part.

POLLY. I'm staying here. I told you.

PAUL. No, you didn't. You said you were coming to town.

POLLY. Well, where did you think I was going to stay?

PAUL. The Plaza. I thought you would stay at the Plaza.

POLLY. We needed to talk.

PAUL. I can talk at the Plaza.

POLLY. Why should I spend all that money when you've got a perfectly good place here? And why don't you ever pick anything up?

PAUL. I was hoping to discourage visitors.

POLLY. There are socks and newspapers all over the floor.

PAUL. Yeah, well, they stop the carpet getting dirty; this way I don't have to vacuum.

POLLY. (*Picking up stack of typescript from floor, down center.*) We'll start picking up now.

PAUL. If you want picking up you should go to the Plaza. (*SHE looks at him.*) That's not what I meant.

POLLY. (*Holding typescript.*) Where does this go?

PAUL. Right there.

POLLY. What d'you mean, right there? I'm standing in the middle of the floor.

PAUL. That's where it goes. That's my novel. I know exactly where it is.

POLLY. Ah, the much discussed and long awaited novel. I suppose I'll have to read it. If we're going to work together, I'd better know what you've been doing. (*Puts it down.*) Y'know, I re-read the first Miss Charlie recently. I can't tell anymore what you wrote and what I wrote.

PAUL. I wrote the good bits.

POLLY. I imagine in the real world the murderer is usually the most likely suspect. I wonder if being messy is a motive for murder?

PAUL. Listen, why don't we start on this nice and fresh first thing tomorrow morning, over coffee, at the Plaza.

POLLY. I'm not staying at the Plaza.

PAUL. The YWCA—wherever.

POLLY. Here. I'm staying here.

PAUL. You can't stay here. I ... I have mice. You hate mice.

POLLY. So do you.

PAUL. I got used to them. They don't tidy.

POLLY. Obviously not. Where's the exercise bicycle?

PAUL. I got rid of the exercise bicycle and I'm in much better shape. I no longer smash my toe into it on the way to the john in the middle of the night.

POLLY. Y'know, there's always the basic obvious motive—money. Speaking of which, what are you living on?

PAUL. (*Defensive.*) If you must know I sometimes work, part-time, in the same bookstore where we met. And I cut out olives. Anyway it's much cheaper living without you and your long distance phone calls to Peggy and Muffy and the dreaded Ellen.

POLLY. You never liked my friends. You had your friends and I had mine and you never liked mine.

PAUL. I sure didn't like them costing us hundreds of dollars a month. Didn't you know anyone local?

POLLY. Not as local as your drinking buddies in the bar downstairs where you spent every bit as much as I did on the phone.

PAUL. At least with me it was pay as you go. You and the trendy, chatty, upscale Vassar gang saved it all for a big surprise at the end of the month. I'd have cheerfully strangled Ellen.

POLLY. I was right: it's money. That's why people murder each other. And that's why I came back here, so we could work together and make some money.

PAUL. And just out of curiosity, not that I give a damn, really, why did you leave in the first place? Was that money?

POLLY. (Beat. Uncertain.) I guess. Sure it was. What else?

PAUL. That's it? Money?

POLLY. They pay a lot for screenplays.

PAUL. Well, you know what you should do with all that money.

POLLY. What?

PAUL. Get a room at the Plaza.

POLLY. We had a room at the Plaza once.

PAUL. One night—that was all we could afford. Our honeymoon.

POLLY. It was the second best night of my life.

PAUL. Oh, yeah? What was the best?

POLLY. The first night here.

PAUL. Here! Really? But we didn't even have a bed here then. Just the sleeping bag on the floor. Talk about uncomfortable.

POLLY. Well, as you said, we used to be young and in love.

PAUL. And now?

POLLY. Now, we don't even have to like each other,

we just have to work together—as fast and efficiently as possible. We'll have coffee here in the morning. I hope you've got orange juice. You can use the sleeping bag. I'll set the alarm, so we can get up early. And we'll start fresh on a brand new murder; *Miss Charlie Rides Again.* It'll be just like the old days. Well, I don't know about you, but I'm exhausted.

PAUL. Me too. (*Heads for bathroom.*)

POLLY. (*As HE goes.*) From the travelling, I guess.

(*PAUL exits.*)

POLLY. I don't think it's the plane. I think it's the bus from the airport and the taxi from the bus stop. (*Calls out.*) Remember to leave the seat down. (*Finds a couple of clean shirts folded from the laundry. Puts them on the round table, moving the pistol gingerly to do so. Picks up some paperbacks.*) Rex Stout. Rex Stout. Community Property. Rex Stout. (*Puts them away.*)

(*PAUL re-enters buttoning a fresh shirt and carrying a toilet kit which he will zip.*)

POLLY. You don't really mind if I straighten up a bit, do you?

PAUL. No, not at all. Go ahead.

POLLY. It'll just make it easier in the morning if the place is in order. What are you doing? Are you getting ready for bed?

PAUL. Yeah, I guess you could say that.

POLLY. Most people take their clothes off.

PAUL. Not if they're going across town. If Sandra

calls, tell her I'm on my way.

POLLY. What?

PAUL. On my way. Across town. Tell her.

POLLY. But I'm here ... I mean, I'm here to work.

PAUL. (*Putting on jacket.*) Don't worry—nine AM. Sharp. And listen, I'm sorry for all the comments about picking up. It's just that when I'm here, it kinda gets on my nerves. But while I'm out is fine. I actually like it clean and tidy. Spotless, I like. So, I mean if you get up before I'm back, go to it. I tell you, when you're through in here, the bathroom really needs help. I mean, you should see the tub. Disgusting. (*Crossing to front door.*) You've been away so long, you know, in California that I've sort of forgotten—let me ask you something: do you do windows?

POLLY. I ... don't believe this!

PAUL. Oh, when you get up in the morning, the toaster isn't working. (*Exits.*)

POLLY. (*Pursuing to door.*) The toaster isn't working! The toaster is the least of it. Nothing's working, including you. It's all out of order. (*Idea.*) Out of order. Out of order. Out of order. (*Which SHE repeats as SHE snatches up a magic marker from the table. Looks around for something to write on. Crosses to desk, picks up a clean shirt, rips it open to get the cardboard.*) Out of order. Out of order. (*Printing huge letters savagely.*) OUT OF ORDER (*Surveys her work.*) Out of order. My whole damn life is out of order.

CURTAIN

Scene 3

*The same. Early the next morning. A blanket and pillow on
the couch indicate someone slept there without opening
it. The stool has been moved down stage to about where
the manuscript was in Scenes 1 and 2. POLLY in an
attractive bathrobe is sitting on the stool with a
manuscript on her lap. Around her feet are scattered
manuscript pages which SHE has apparently let go so
they flutter down. SHE picks up each page individually
to read it. SHE is reading a page now. There is no
indication that she is enjoying it. SHE opens her fingers
and the page flutters down. SHE picks up the next page
and reads. The front door is opened by PAUL. HE is as
we saw him last, with the Dopp kit, but the sweater or
jacket has been taken off and trails from his hand. HE
leans against the door jamb for support. HE is very
seriously out of breath. Gasps for a moment. then
heaves himself into the room, closing the door.*

POLLY. (*Without looking up.*) Did you have a hard
night?

PAUL. (*Gasping.*) Elevator ... out-of ... order ...
Seven flights ... seven ... Thank God, we don't have a
stoop ... There *are* four steps in the lobby ... When I got to
... (*Gasping, holds up seven fingers.*) Elevator opened ...
You ... you did it ... It was my idea and ... you took it! ...
if I die, it's a steal from Christie ... if I live and I may, it's
a steal from Neil Simon ... Either way, I resent being got
with my very own idea.

POLLY. (*Flatly, without looking up.*) There's coffee.

And I fixed the toaster. I plugged it in.

PAUL. (*Sarcastically.*) Oh, very ... (*Too breathless to finish. Pushes himself toward kitchen.*) If I'd wanted to feel like this, I'd have kept the exercise bicycle. (*HE exits kitchen.*)

(*As the kitchen door closes, POLLY throws both arms in the air and shakes her fists in triumph, a silent "gotcha." Reverts to reading instantly. PAUL re-enters with coffee mug.*)

PAUL. So? What are you doing?

(*POLLY does not reply.*)

PAUL. Reading? (*Beat.*) What're you reading? (*No reply. PAUL comes closer to her to see what SHE is reading. Note that in all this reading sequence PAUL is behind, i.e., Upstage of Polly.*) You're reading my novel. (*Beat.*) Good. (*Beat.*) I think.

(*HE is very close to her. At this point SHE again opens her fingers. HE watches as the page flutters down. PAUL always waits until a page has landed. After it has landed.*)

PAUL. Like it? (*Moves back a step or two.*) It's sort of autobiographical. About us. From real life. (*A page drops. PAUL rushes up.*) Wow! That was fast. (*Looks down at page on floor.*) Oh, that page. Yeah, well, I guess we didn't have real life that day. (*Moves away. Following sequence not rushed.*) What do you think?... It's good, I think ...

Not great, good ... Well, maybe it's not all good, not yet ... But I like it. Pretty much. Most of it ... (*A page drops.*) I mean, that's a first draft you have there ... I plan to fix it ... (*A page drops. Defensive.*) Okay, so it's not perfect. You have a few little reservations. That's natural. That's natural.

POLLY. This isn't from real life; real life doesn't take this long.

PAUL. That's me!

POLLY. (*Looks up for first time.*) Oh, Paul, I'm so sorry. It must be hell to go through life in sentence fragments.

(*POLLY resumes reading. PAUL breaks away to the closet. Opens closet, which is crammed, and finally drags out a shotgun. Takes it to couch. Carefully and quietly breaks gun. Squints up barrel. Blows up barrel. Closes gun. Puts gun down. Crosses to sideboard and open drawer. Returns to couch with ball of string and a shotgun shell. Measures a yard from nose to outstretched finger tips. Four yards. Breaks string. Hurts hand.*)

POLLY. (*Without looking up.*) There are four "esses" in scissors. (*Continues reading.*)

(*PAUL carefully and neatly ties a tiny loop in one end of string. Threads other end. Pulls until HE has a tiny noose. Slips noose over trigger. Cocks hammer.*)

POLLY. Well, Heaven knows, I've found the deadly part. I'm still reading for coherence.

(PAUL pulls string. Click. Checks to see if she has noticed. SHE has not. HE smiles. Re-breaks gun. Puts it down. Empties shot from shotgun shell. Carefully inserts shell in breach. Carefully closes gun.)

POLLY. If I'd been here, I'd have fixed these comma faults.

(PAUL crosses to kitchen with gun, trailing string. As HE goes.)

POLLY. But not with semi-colons. You've used up all the semicolons in the world. *(PAUL has exited. POLLY pauses in her reading to stretch. Checks with horror the still sizable pile of typescript to be read. Mutters.)* How long, Oh Lord, how long? *(Resumes reading.)*

PAUL. *(Re-enters backwards, slowly and carefully from the kitchen, letting the door close very gently. Pleased with himself. Crosses, sits and sips coffee.)* Coffee's still hot. If you'd like to go and get some.

(POLLY reads.)

PAUL. And as you said, the toaster's working. You could make some toast. In the kitchen.

POLLY. Does anyone ever get killed in this book? This is plotless.

PAUL. Sometimes that's how things are.

POLLY. Listen, if I want plotless or pointless I can stick with real life. In a book or onstage I want something to happen. I want the gun to go off.

PAUL. It'll go off. Don't worry, I promise you the gun will go off.

POLLY. I don't suppose there's any chance it will hit Cassandra. Cassandra. Sandra. Well, I wonder who that little nymphomaniac could be? She reads like an adolescent sex phantasy. No wonder you were out of breath and hot and bothered; you must have had quite a night.

PAUL. Just for the record, she had a throbbing headache last night.

POLLY. Oh, dear, and you put on a nice, clean shirt. Well, never mind, you can make the rest of it up. You've made up so much already.

PAUL. I didn't make that up. That's from real life. I told you she was agile.

POLLY. Agile! I don't care if the little tramp is a circus contortionist. You're not. I've been there and I know. You're not that agile.

PAUL. Yes, I am! I mean, I have to be careful of my back, y'know, it could go at any time. But I am. Agile. Sometimes.

POLLY. From real life—you wish! I'm only pointing out these things because you're a professional writer and I'm a professional writer and you want a professional opinion, don't you?

PAUL. Not really, no.

POLLY. Of course, you do. I mean, we're adults, aren't we?

PAUL. Not that adult. Let me tell you something: there isn't a writer living who finishes something and wants a calm, reasoned, professional opinion. I didn't give up friends and meals and beer and sunlight for a professional opinion.

POLLY. What do you want?

PAUL. I want you to like it.

POLLY. Well, that's enough about your novel. (*Puts it down.*) It's nine o'clock; time for us to get to work. Now I'm working on a plot and I have an idea that a character, A, goes to visit another character, B, who lives in a place like this. Character A needs to find an incriminating document in the apartment. A letter, a will, a scrap of paper.

PAUL. A scrap of paper is the oldest theatrical device in the world.

POLLY. Good. That means it works. Now A and B hardly know each other.

PAUL. We're perfect casting.

POLLY. Let's say they're mutual friends. So how does A, in order to search the room, get it to him or herself?

PAUL. He or she could scream fire, fire!

POLLY. (*Ignoring.*) Maybe A asks for something. What do you ask for when you're in someone else's home?

PAUL. The remote control for the TV and a beer.

POLLY. A glass of water. That's reasonable. A glass of water.

PAUL. Why? Are they out of beer?

POLLY. A glass of water is perfect. (*Sits.*) Ready? (*Acting.*) Excuse me, may I have a glass of water, please.

PAUL. Sure. Go ahead.

POLLY. (*Patiently.*) Let's try that again. I'm A; you're B. You have to go and get it for me so I can search the room. Excuse me, may I have a glass of water, please.

PAUL. (*Crosses to kitchen.*) A glass of water? Sure, no problem. In fact, I may join you. I'm a little thirsty. (*At*

*kitchen door, poised to exit, remembers gun. Freezes.) Er
... You're sure you want a glass of water?*

POLLY. Yes, please.

PAUL. Er ... Did you want ice in it?

POLLY. No, thank you, just plain water.

PAUL. Okay. *(Very fast cross to bathroom.)* Glass of
water. Coming right up. *(Exits bathroom.)*

*(As soon as HE exits, POLLY jumps up and rushes to table
DL and starts searching. Moves papers and pistol, so
audience sees pistol. PAUL re-enters with a glass of
water almost instantaneously.)*

PAUL. Hey! What are you doing going through my
things?

POLLY. You were much to fast. Why did you go the
bathroom?

PAUL. To get you a glass of water.

POLLY. The water's in the kitchen.

PAUL. It's the same water.

POLLY. Any normal person would go to the kitchen. I
have to search the room.

PAUL. It's just a glass of water.

POLLY. Well, take more time.

PAUL. It doesn't take more time to fill a little glass of
water.

POLLY. Fill a bigger glass.

PAUL. I'd have to fill the bathtub.

POLLY. Okay, I've got it. You mentioned ice. That's
it. Then you'll have to go to the kitchen and get ice out of
the trays. *(Sits.)* Yes, please, a glass of *ice* water.

PAUL. *(Fast.)* We're out of ice.

POLLY. No, we're not.

PAUL. Yes, we are.

POLLY. I saw ice in there this morning.

PAUL. I used it.

POLLY. When?

PAUL. When ... When I came in all hot from climbing the stairs and went in the kitchen. I used the ice to cool down.

POLLY. Well, *pretend* there's ice. Show some initiative, for Heaven's sake.

PAUL. (*Hands her glass.*) Listen, if you want to make getting a glass of water a major event, you do it. I'll be A and you be B. And you can pretend there's ice in the kitchen.

(*SHE crosses to kitchen.*)

PAUL. This way I get to sit around and give orders and you get to fetch and carry.

POLLY. (*With hand on kitchen door, stops.*) I guess a glass of water doesn't take very long. Maybe we should use something else?

PAUL. No, no, water's fine. Go ahead. You're right there.

POLLY. Maybe B could offer coffee?

PAUL. Coffee's good, that'll work, it's in the kitchen.

POLLY. But I want the idea to come from A. What could you ask for that would take some time?

PAUL. Lobster thermidor.

POLLY. Paul, you are giving me a headache.

PAUL. Well, take an aspirin.

POLLY. That's it! Aspirin is it. It's perfectly

reasonable for a visitor to ask for a glass of water and some aspirin. A asks for aspirin. (*Pauses.*) Paul, ask for aspirin.

PAUL. (*Mechanically.*) May I have some aspirin and a glass of water, please?

POLLY. (*Crossing to bathroom.*) Oh, of course. I won't be a moment.

PAUL. Where are you going?

POLLY. I'm going to get the aspirin.

PAUL. It's not there. It's in the kitchen.

POLLY. It's in the bathroom.

PAUL. It's in the kitchen.

POLLY. No, it's not.

PAUL. Yes, it is. It's in the kitchen.

POLLY. We've always kept it in the bathroom.

PAUL. We?! What d'you mean we? We don't live here anymore. I live here. And the aspirin's in the kitchen.

POLLY. Why?

PAUL. Why? It just is. It's my kitchen and my aspirin and I put them together.

POLLY. (*Crossing to kitchen.*) Oh, all right. But we always kept the aspirin in the bathroom, because that's where they put the medicine cabinet.

PAUL. You can never find anything in a medicine cabinet—it's always full of old Dristan and the wrong size Band-Aids.

POLLY. (*At kitchen door.*) This is the wrong glass. This place is completely disorganized. (*Crossing to bathroom.*) The aspirin is supposed to be in the bathroom with the Q-Tips, not in the kitchen with the Alka-Seltzer.

PAUL. (*Exasperated.*) Where are you going?

POLLY. (*Stopped.*) This is the glass from the bathroom. I'm going to put it back in the bathroom.

PAUL. It doesn't matter.

POLLY. Yes, it does.

PAUL. No, it doesn't. Go in the kitchen. You are driving me crazy.

POLLY. Of course, it matters. If I were going to get you aspirin from the kitchen, I wouldn't go and get the glass from the bathroom first. The bathroom glass would be in the bathroom, where it belongs, and the drinking glasses would be in the kitchen where they belong.

PAUL. Are we rehearsing a murder or re-staging our marriage?

POLLY. If we were re-staging our marriage, the aspirin would be in the bathroom where it belongs.

PAUL. If I put this in my novel, no one would believe it.

POLLY. *(Puts water down.)* No one's going to believe anything in your novel anyway.

PAUL. Oh, really, why not?

POLLY. I'll tell you why not. *(Picking up novel manuscript.)* The three main characters are completely unbelievable. There's a very flattering, self-serving portrait of the author, who, I should like to point out, did not even get into Princeton let alone on a football scholarship; there's Cassandra, the erotic goddess; and the wife, the Wicked Witch of the West, me.

PAUL. It's only a novel.

POLLY. I should also like to point out that I did not strip the car gears on purpose. I did strip the car gears. But not on purpose. I did not have an affair with the Italian across the hall. And I did not set off for California without a word leaving you to starve.

PAUL. You took all the bologna.

POLLY. No, I did not. There was one slice of bologna left and I very carefully cut it in half.

PAUL. You what?

POLLY. I cut it in half.

PAUL. Community property does not include bologna. Gee, I'm hungry. What would I like? How about a one half of one slice of bologna sandwich? That should fill me right up. Yum, yum!

POLLY. I was trying to be fair.

PAUL. Fair! Fair does not apply to bologna. When Solomon in his wisdom said cut it in half, he wasn't talking about bologna. Babies, yes; bologna, no.

POLLY. And another thing: I did not drive you to drink. Take some credit: you did that all by yourself.

PAUL. Well, since you split, I've done everything all by myself.

POLLY. Including your own punctuation.

PAUL. (*Serious.*) You hate my novel, don't you?

POLLY. You hate your characters.

PAUL. Just one of them.

POLLY. This is a hatchet job—an angry bitter novel.

PAUL. It started light and amusing, then it turned angry and bitter as I put in everything I know.

POLLY. Well, it's all wrong. You have made me a monster.

PAUL. It's the truth.

POLLY. (*Tossing the remaining manuscript up in the air so that it cascades everywhere.*) It's baloney!

PAUL. (*After it's all settled. Stunned.*) That's my life. All over the floor.

POLLY. You said that's were you kept it.

PAUL. It's a mess.

POLLY. It's your life. Did you ever think of picking it up and straightening it out?

PAUL. It's my best work.

POLLY. It's not good enough.

PAUL. It's my very best work.

POLLY. And, it's not good enough.

PAUL. (*Explaining.*) It's everything I know.

POLLY. (*Implacable.*) It's not good enough.

(Pause.)

PAUL. (*Advancing on her.*) I wouldn't work with you if it would cure the common cold.

POLLY. (*SHE backs to round table.*) You're overreacting.

PAUL. Overreacting? I'm going to kill you. How's that for overreacting?

POLLY. Don't take it personally. It's just an opinion.

PAUL. Don't take it personally? Whaddaya mean, don't take it personally! Your life is not good enough, don't take it personally. That's not an opinion, that's a motive for murder! How very convenient that you're in California, and you covered your tracks. There's no record of your ever being here. (*Putting his hands around her throat.*) I'm not only going to enjoy this. I'm going to get away with it.

(Groping behind her on the desk, POLLY has found the pistol.)

PAUL. The perfect murder. And no busybody Miss Charlie around to solve it.

*(SHE puts the gun up to his head. PAUL drops his hands
    from her throat and backs Center fast.)*

PAUL. That's a real gun! Don't shoot! That's real! I
was only kidding.

*(SHE fires. Three times. BANG BANG BANG. PAUL
    flinches and clutches his torso.)*

PAUL. Oh, my God, you've done it this time.

*(POLLY advances to Center. PAUL staggers backwards to
    Down Right. SHE fires again. Three times. BANG
    BANG BANG. PAUL slumps on chair Down Right.)*

POLLY. This place is such a mess. I think I'll check
into the Plaza.
PAUL. *(Discovering he is not dead.)* No holes. No
blood.
POLLY. *(Lofting gun.)* No slugs. I changed them last
night.
PAUL. I need an aspirin! *(Rushes to kitchen and exits.
From the kitchen there is a huge SHOTGUN EXPLOSION
and as the door swings back, SMOKE billows out.)*
POLLY. Gotcha!

CURTAIN

ACT II

Scene 4

The same. Friday evening. The apartment has been tidied and cleaned up.

For this Act, in which the actions should be mostly concentrated front and center, the position of the sofa-bed may have been re-adjusted. It should be placed so that when open on the diagonal only a fairly narrow strip exists in front of the downstage corner, but sufficient to play. The chest is re-positioned, with lid opening away from the audience, so that when the bed opens the DR side of the bed will be flush with the side of the chest. The stool is in the way of the bed opening. The desk chair is Center of the round table. This group may be cheated slightly center.

PAUL is dressed differently but similarly to Act I. POLLY is in slacks or jeans and a top. SHE carries a large handbag. THEY are near the door, kissing. It is a friendly and matrimonial, not a sexy, kiss. As THEY break.

PAUL. Love you lots.

POLLY. Love you much.

PAUL. Don't be long.

POLLY. Won't be long. (*POLLY opening front-door.*)

PAUL. Remember, all you have to do, using the keys as an excuse, is get my fingerprints on the pill bottle.

45

Fingerprints.

(POLLY exits front door.

PAUL counters DL. Immediately a KNOCKING at the front door. PAUL crosses and opens it. POLLY enters and crosses into room looking around.)

PAUL. Hello, darling. That didn't take long.

POLLY. Have you seen my keys, darling? I forgot my keys.

PAUL. Where did you leave them, darling.

POLLY. Well, if I knew that, I wouldn't have lost them, darling.

PAUL. In the kitchen, dear.

POLLY. I know I never had them in the kitchen, darling.

PAUL. Bathroom, dear?

POLLY. I don't think so, darling.

PAUL. You're always losing your keys.

POLLY. I know, I feel like such a goose, darling.

PAUL. And where do you generally find them, dear?

POLLY. I don't know. Where do I generally find them?

PAUL. In your handbag, darling, in your handbag.

POLLY. *(Starts to rummage in the very large, obviously full handbag.)* You know, I think you're right. Gosh, I can't find them, darling.

PAUL. What have you got in there?

POLLY. Oh, you know, just things.

PAUL. Let me help you, darling.

POLLY. No, I can ...

PAUL. I *want* to help you, darling.

POLLY. Oh, all right, darling. Can darling hold these,

please darling? (*Hands him a hairbrush, a prescription pill bottle and a billfold. Rummages.*)

PAUL. I think I can manage that, dear.

POLLY. Let me see ... Maybe they're under ... Guess what I've found. (*Produces keys.*)

PAUL. What did I tell you.

POLLY. You know best, darling. (*Starts to cross to door.*) Well, I'm off again.

. PAUL. Darling ...

POLLY. What?

PAUL. Didn't we forget something, dear?

POLLY. (*With keys.*) No, I have them now.

PAUL. Darling, kiss, kiss.

POLLY. (*Crossing back.*) Sorry, sorry. (*Gives him a sweet peck.*)

PAUL. Love you lots.

POLLY. Love you much.

PAUL. Don't be long.

POLLY. Won't be long. (*POLLY exits.*)

(*PAUL is still holding the pill bottle, billfold and hairbrush. With a trace of irritation, HE puts the brush and billfold on the table and holds the pill bottle up. POLLY enters—SHE has used her key—in doorway.*)

POLLY. Okay. How was that ... (*Trails off as SHE sees the pill bottle PAUL holds up. Crosses briskly to him, snatches the pill bottle out of his hand, and crosses back to the door, throwing the pill bottle in her purse. At the open front door as SHE takes her keys from the lock.*)

PAUL. Remember, all you have to do ...

POLLY. I know, fingerprints. (*Exits closing front*

door.)

(Immediately KNOCKING on door. PAUL to door. Movement, business repeats. This time it is all just barely noticeably faster and crisper.)

PAUL. Hello, darling. That didn't take long.

POLLY. Have you seen my keys, darling? I forgot my keys.

PAUL. Well, where did you leave them, kitten?

POLLY. Well, if I knew that, I wouldn't have lost them, sugar.

PAUL. In the kitchen, honey?

POLLY. I know I never had them in the kitchen, honeybunch.

PAUL. Bathroom, honeybuns?

POLLY. I don't think so, sweetheart.

PAUL. You're forever losing your keys.

POLLY. Silly, silly me.

PAUL. And where do we generally find them, sweetie?

POLLY. I forget, sweetface.

PAUL. In your handbag, sweetcakes, in your handbag.

POLLY. Oh, gee, that's right. Silly snookums. *(Rummages as before.)* Gosh. I can't find them.

PAUL. What all have you got in there?

POLLY. Oh, you know, just things, Tiger.

PAUL. Let me help you, sweet pea.

POLLY. No, I can …

PAUL. I *want* to help you.

POLLY. Oh, all right. Can you hold these, sweetie pie? *(Hands him pill bottle, compact, scarf, address book and hairspray.)*

PAUL. I think I can manage that, sweet lips.

POLLY. Let me see ... Maybe they're under ... Eureka, eureka. (*Produces keys.*)

PAUL. What did I tell you?

POLLY. You know best, sweet cheeks. (*Pointedly takes pill bottle out of his hand—will put it in bag.*) Well, I'm off again. (*Starts cross to door.*)

PAUL. Sweet potato pie ...

POLLY. What?

PAUL. Didn't we forget something?

POLLY. (*With keys.*) No, I have them now. And the pill bottle.

PAUL. Plant a big, sloppy, wet one right here.

POLLY. You're not serious.

PAUL. (*Pained.*) Sugar lips!

(*SHE gives him a biggish kiss, but body language not in it.*)

PAUL. Love you lots.

POLLY. Love you much.

PAUL. Don't be long.

POLLY. Won't be long. (*POLLY exits.*)

(*PAUL exasperated dumps the handbag stuff on the table. POLLY using her keys which SHE leaves in the lock, re-enters. SHE holds the pill bottle.*)

POLLY. Okay, I got the pill bottle. And the fingerprints.

PAUL. Whose fingerprints?

POLLY. (*Snaps.*) Well your fingerprints, of course! I remember taking it out of your ... (*POLLY realizes.*) Oh.

PAUL. (*Patiently.*) Listen up, use your little grey cells, this is how it works. You come in: you've lost your keys. You search the handbag, handing me stuff including the pill bottle. You find the keys. You have the keys in one hand, the handbag in the other, both hands full, so you hold out the open, gaping handbag and I toss everything back in including the pill bottle with my fingerprints. Get it?

POLLY. Got it.

PAUL. Good.

(POLLY exits front door. Immediate KNOCKING, PAUL to door. Movement, business repeats. Faster, crisper but don't lose variations.)

PAUL. Hello, darling. This is taking longer than I could possibly have imagined.

POLLY. Have you seen my keys, darling. I forgot my keys.

(BOTH are very, very bright and friendly.)

PAUL. Well, where did you leave them, dearest?

POLLY. Well, if I knew that I wouldn't have lost them, dear heart.

PAUL. In the kitchen, pudding?

POLLY. I know I never had them in the kitchen, pumpkin.

PAUL. Bathroom, light of my life?

POLLY. I don't think so, my reason for living.

PAUL. You're forever losing your keys.

POLLY. I guess, I'm just a scatterbrain.

PAUL. And where do we generally find them,

babycakes?

POLLY. I forget, Daddy.

PAUL. In your handbag, lamb chop, in your handbag.

POLLY. (*Rummages as before.*) Oh, gee, that's right. I'm a moron. Gosh, I can't find them.

PAUL. What all have you got in there?

POLLY. A lot less than I started with.

PAUL. Let me help you, muffin.

POLLY. No, I can ...

PAUL. I *want* to help you.

POLLY. Oh, all right. (*Will hand him in this order: flashlight, airline ticket, half-eaten candy bar, handkerchief, packet of condoms, length of clothesline, pill bottle.*) Can the big strong man hold these?

PAUL. I think I can manage that, cutey.

POLLY. (*Rummages.*) Let me see ...

PAUL. (*Reading.*) "Extra-pleasure, extra-strength, pre-lubricated. Assorted colors." These are condoms. What are you doing with ... And a rope!? My God, you've changed.

POLLY. Clothesline. We're gonna need one. Maybe they're under ... Well, they were right here.

PAUL. This is kinky. You were never into kinky. Were you?

POLLY. I can't find them.

PAUL. What?

POLLY. The keys. I've really lost them.

PAUL. You can't have. You just had them.

POLLY. I know I just had them.

PAUL. Well, where did you leave them? (*Continues to hold stuff.*)

POLLY. If I knew where I'd left them, they wouldn't be lost, dummy.

PAUL. In the kitchen?

POLLY. Did you see me go to the kitchen, birdbrain?

PAUL. Bathroom? You spend hours in the bathroom; maybe they're in the bathroom.

POLLY. They're not in the bathroom. I know where things are in the bathroom. I even know where things are which should be in the bathroom that are in the kitchen, you jerk.

PAUL. You retarded cretin. You're forever loosing the Goddamned keys. You'd lose your head if it wasn't screwed on.

POLLY. Oh, very witty.

PAUL. (*Crosses to front door.*) You can't find them, and now you've cleaned up in here, we'll never find anything ever again. I don't know why I'm doing this. I said I wasn't going to work with you. (*PAUL opens front door and checks for keys which are not there. Returns.*)

POLLY. You're doing it so you can get your hands on that wretched car and fix it up.

PAUL. And now you've lost keys you were holding moments, *moments* ago. Did you put them down?

POLLY. No, I didn't put them down.

PAUL. Then they've got to be in your bag. Look in your bag.

POLLY. They're not in my bag.

PAUL. Will you look! Under the stuff.

POLLY. What stuff?

PAUL. The sexual accessories!

POLLY. (*Holding bag out with both hands to show him.*) The bag is empty! You're holding the stuff, meathead.

PAUL. (*Slamming the things HE is holding into the*

bag.) Unbelievable! You are terminally stupid. (*Slamming things from table back into bag, one by one. The silk scarf will get left on the table.*) Well, stuff this! Here take back your extra-pleasure, extra-strength, pre-lubricated, sprayed, combed and painted, big-screenwriter, California life-style in assorted colors. I have to tell you when I use those the choice between purple and mocha is the last thing on my mind. I hope to God, that's a return ticket. Can't you do anything right?

POLLY. *(Beat.)* Well, I did get the pill bottle with your fingerprints on it back in the bag.

PAUL. Oh. So you did. That's very good. Then where are the keys?

POLLY. In my pocket. If they're in her pocket she has to empty the entire bag.

PAUL. That's fantastic.

POLLY. Thank you. See we can work together.

PAUL. Didn't we forget something, sex-puppy?

POLLY. What?

PAUL. Gimme some tongue, babe.

POLLY. No way, Sandra's Little Gummy Bear.

PAUL. (*Big. Street. Go for it.*) Honey-sugar-sweetie-baby. My own delicious little packet of yellow cake mix with a rich, moist puddin' already in the box, so good you don't need frosting, eat it all up, put your face down and lick that plate squeaky clean.

POLLY. Paul, that is precisely why you didn't get into Princeton.

PAUL. Love you lots.

POLLY. What?

PAUL. (*Sheepish.*) Just sticking to the script.

POLLY. Well, we've established how she can get his

fingerprints on the bottle. That's done. Where are the plot notes? We'll check it off.

PAUL. Does that mean it's quittin' time?

POLLY. No, it doesn't. We've only been working a couple of hours.

PAUL. Listen, if being a writer meant a hard eight hour day, I'd have chosen something lighter—the Department of Motor Vehicles or the Post Office.

POLLY. (*With a list on table.*) We've really only got one more big thing to check today.

PAUL. What's that?

POLLY. The scene where the girl, who took sleeping pills the night before, wakes up in bed to find that her hands are tied behind her back, there's a corpse with a knife in it and her only way out is to crawl to the body and cut the ropes on the protruding knife.

PAUL. Repeat that.

POLLY. Girl tied up in bed—corpse with knife in it— crawl to body—cut ropes on murder weapon.

PAUL. It's so lurid, so Mickey Spillane. What happened to clues and detection? Whatever happened to deduction?

POLLY. It's illegal in Hollywood. We have to be visual, visual, visual and give them a couple of big scenes. And for this big scene we need a sharp knife.

(PAUL starts to kitchen.)

POLLY. I'll open the sofa bed. We've got a rope. It shouldn't take long.

PAUL. You're sure this is going to make enough money to fix the car?

POLLY. (*Starting on sofa-bed.*) With a long blade, please, Paul.

(*HE exits. Moves stool so it abuts chest stage R. SHE takes the two main cushions off the sofa-bed and places them on the floor, Down Stage Center. Note: the sofa-bed should ideally be one such that only the two seat cushions need to be removed. SHE opens the sofa-bed. PAUL re-enters from the kitchen with a long knife, a pitcher of martinis and two glasses. All of which HE will set down.*)

PAUL. You know, I'm not absolutely sure it's possible to be a professional writer without olives.

POLLY. You don't even pour that till we've done this.

PAUL. (*Indicating chest.*) I generally put the cushions on there.

POLLY. (*Arranging cushions.*) This is the body.

PAUL. Should go to the gym more often.

POLLY. (*Getting rope from her bag.*) Heigh ho, heigh ho, it's off to work we go.

PAUL. And to think my parents wanted me to be an orthodontist.

POLLY. My parents wanted me to marry one.

PAUL. Oh, good, we've disappointed everybody.

POLLY. Put your hands behind your back.

PAUL. Wait a minute. Flip you for it—heads I win, tails you lose.

(*POLLY deadpans.*)

PAUL. Well, it's not fair, I've already been stabbed,

strangled, forced up seven flights, and shot. Anyway, it's
supposed to be a girl. Put your hands behind your back.

POLLY. Oh, all right, get on with it. *(As HE ties her
hands.)* Not too tight.

PAUL. It's got to be tight enough to work. How's that?

POLLY. Okay. I think it's okay. I won't be like this for
long, will I?

PAUL. No—ooo! Now hop on the bed.

(SHE sits on bed.)

PAUL. And, sort of, turn on your side and bend your
knees.

POLLY. *(Wary.)* Why?

PAUL. So I can tie your ankles.

POLLY. I don't think her ankles are tied.

PAUL. Sure they are.

POLLY. Then how's she gonna get to the corpse?

PAUL. *(Tying her ankles.)* With great difficulty. Don't
worry about visual; I think we've got visual covered.

POLLY. *(Sharply.)* Paul, are you enjoying this?

PAUL. *(HE is.)* Of course not. Does he torture her?

POLLY. No, he does not torture her.

PAUL. Well, you can't have everything. There, that
should do it.

*(POLLY is tied up thus—hands tied together behind back,
rope from hands to ankles which are tied together.
There should, of course, be more play in the rope than
the actress shows or the audience sees.)*

POLLY. I can't move.

PAUL. Sure you can.

(POLLY will struggle to an upright position, i.e. on her knees. This is not easy.)

POLLY. Paul, I can't move.

PAUL. *(Crossing to knife.)* You can't play badminton; you can move. The body is female, right?

POLLY. Right.

PAUL. Then, let me see. *(Crosses to closet, where HE will get Polly's bathrobe.)* Gee, I haven't had this much fun since we cut up the cow.

POLLY. This is obviously not going to work. It was a bad idea. It was my idea and a bad idea. I take it back. She'll never make it. It doesn't work. We'll have to think of something else. I'm sorry. You can untie me now. I said, you can untie me now.

(During the above, PAUL has returned DC with the bathrobe. HE shakes out the bathrobe and drapes it over the seat cushions. HE places Polly's handbag at the head of the "body.")

PAUL. You can make it. There. Almost lifelike. *(Drives knife into floor between cushions.)* Take your best shot. Remember, you always had faith in me? Well, Polly, I have faith in you. *(Has backed off.)* Go for it!

POLLY. Paul, untie me at once. *(Pause.)* If you don't untie me at once, I'll scream. *(Realizes.)* That's it! That's it! What would she do? She'd scream for help. Okay, you can untie me now, the plan won't work.

PAUL. *(PAUL is right where the silk scarf was left. HE*

casually picks it up.) Sure it will. See, it's important that we rehearse these things—find the flaws, work out the kinks, plug the holes. Especially plug the holes.

POLLY. What is that?

PAUL. It's a scarf.

POLLY. I know it's a scarf. What are you doing with it?

PAUL. I'm gonna stop you screaming for help.

POLLY. (*Dangerously.*) You wouldn't dare.

PAUL. Bound and gagged. They go together. Makes perfect sense.

POLLY. She is not gagged.

PAUL. Tell me something, is the murderer a married man?

POLLY. Yes.

PAUL. She's gagged.

POLLY. She is not gagged. She is not gagged. She is not ... (*SHE is gagged. Note: for the sake of the actress, only the scarf is used but from the moment of being gagged POLLY is effectively silenced, as if SHE were more thoroughly gagged.*)

PAUL. There. That's perfect. Now all you have to do is climb down, crawl around, get to the body and cut the ropes on the knife. Take your time; there's no rush. Are you ready? Don't answer that. Only watch that first step, it's a big one.

(*PAUL sits. POLLY's movements are going, essentially, to be these: SHE comes to the foot of the bed, looks down and realizes SHE can not get down there. Returns up the bed, goes to the side of the bed furthest from Paul and gets down there. This is quite difficult. SHE will be*

*behind the chest and possibly other obstructions which,
with her hands tied, SHE can not move. So SHE has a
long odyssey to get down front center where the "body"
is. SHE is tied such that SHE can take only the tiniest
steps on her knees and her progress is excruciatingly
slow. The actress will have knee pads under her
trousers. SHE will occasionally have to pause.
Although HE is speaking to her, PAUL's focus is not
principally on her. PAUL's sequence is not played as a
drunk scene, until and as indicated.)*

PAUL. (*Pours both glasses.*) I'll have your drink here
ready for you. (*Unthinkingly tosses off a martini in one
gulp.*) I'll wait for you so we can have our drinks together.
(*Pours refill.*) God, I love doing research. Now, let me see,
what else is on the list? Hey, I'm through for the day. Now
then, what shall ... Here we are. *A Deadly Coherence* by
Paul Butler. Sounds good. Page one, chapter one. (*Reads.
Is bored. Drops page. His reading business parallels
Polly's in Act I, but is not as extended.*) Well, hell, I don't
have to start at the beginning. I wrote it; it's about me; I
know the beginning. I can start anywhere. Except the
ending, I don't know the ending yet. (*Takes page from the
middle. Reads. A page drops.*) This sucks. (*Repeat
business.*) This really sucks. (*Repeat business.*) My God,
I've had a boring life. (*Puts manuscript down.*) I never
really wanted to write a serious novel. It was just
something I used to say, sort of a false lead, a red herring.
You gotta be careful about those things you say, you don't
really mean, or real life is all red herrings. Like if I were to
say something dumb like "Okay, go to California if you
want to, whaddo I care?" That's a red herring. There's a

perception that writers understand things, but the truth may
be that writers understand even less than everyone else,
and that's why they write. To try and understand just what
the hell is going on. Know what I mean? (*Drinks martini
and automatically refills.*) Anyway, when you went west
and I was alone, what else was there to do but write the
damned novel, and drink, of course. I found I had more
time to drink. And think, of course. About our marriage. I
nearly called that (*Manuscript.*) *Marriage Is Murder* but
marriage is murder is redundant. Or was in our case.
(*Beat.*) There were things I missed about our being
together. Don't get me wrong, I don't mean marriage, big
deal. I mean working together, plotting together—some
rainy nights we'd sit here with a pepperoni pizza, slitting
throats. That was the best. The Butlers did it! We made a
little money and we had a lot of fun. (*Sipping.*) And you
know what I miss most—olives! I can't believe I'm out of
olives. This is the drink of a starving artist. How's yours?
(*Drinks hers.*) Same way. Wait a minute. There's a lemon.
I've still got lemon. You like a twist, right? Don't answer
that. (*Rises.*) You just keep marching along there like a
good little soldier, and I'll get us some lemon. (*Exits
kitchen.*)

(*POLLY is almost to the body. PAUL re-enters
    immediately with lemon, tossing it. There is now the
    very faintest indication the drinks are taking effect. Do
    not overdo it.*)

PAUL. Here we are, lemon peel coming up. Hey, look
at you! Good going! It's going to work. Your idea is going
to work! Well done. All you have left to do is cut your

cords and we've got us a big scene. Aren't you proud of
yourself? Don't answer that. Two strips of lemon and we'll
have a celebration. (*Tries casually and unsuccessfully to
get lemon peel with his thumbnail.*) You know, it's good to
be working again. And look how well we're getting on. No
fighting. You said we needed to talk and guess what?
We're talking. And you know what's great about it: I
haven't heard an angry word out of you. Not one.

(*POLLY having reached the "body," has turned around so
that with her hands behind her SHE can reach its knife.
SHE is there.*)

PAUL. This lemon is fighting back. (*In one smooth
movement PAUL plucks the knife from between Polly's
searching fingers and moves to the table to cut the peel.*) I
feel good about us. *Miss Charlie Strikes Again*! How's
that?

(*Twists peel. POLLY starting to turn back around.*)

PAUL. There we are. A new mystery, a new book, it's
like having a baby. Wait a minute. (*Crosses to sideboard.*)
Wait a minute. Having a baby. Where was it? (*Rummages
and produces from sideboard a huge cigar, which HE
brings back down and will light.*) Having a baby. Here we
are. Now who was this? Fellepelle. That's it. Tommy
Fellepelle's kid. So here we are. Together again. Almost
like we were still married.

(*POLLY is now facing front. BOTH are Down Center.*)

PAUL. Funny thing about marriage. Considering the alternative, and I have lived the alternative, marriage ain't so bad. Marriage can be wonderful!

(SHE kneels bound and gagged at his feet. HE looms above her, martini in one hand, huge cigar in the other, swaying slightly. HE exhales a puff of cigar smoke.)

PAUL. I mean, look at us!

CURTAIN

Scene 5

As before. The drinks and the "cushion corpse" have been tidied away. POLLY alone on stage, dressed as before. SHE is on the phone. Sitting on the chest.

POLLY. ... so I'll be there at one-fourteen, Ellen. One-fourteen your time. California, here I come ... Yes, yes, I just got it confirmed on TWA. See you then ... What? No, I'm not going to change my mind ... I know I have to decide what I want out of life, Ellen, and I want you to meet me at the airport ... One-fourteen, LAX, TWA, bye. *(Hangs up. Gets up. The LID of the chest starts to rise. Goes to closet, gets suitcase out, puts it down DR chair, crosses back to phone, brings it down to chest. Dials long distance. Sits on chest. On phone.)* Hello, Ellen. Ellen, it's me again ... No, I can't call Peggy or Muffy. Peggy and

Muffy are both busy ... Who cares, it's his phone bill; I
only wish I had friends in Copenhagen ... What do you
mean get a life; I've got a life, this is it, why do you think
I'm calling in the middle of the night?... I decided what I
want out of life. I want to write another Miss Charlie book,
but I don't think that's going to happen ... Because of
Paul. He's been on again and off again. And right now he's
off again, probably permanently off again ... He said
they're formula stories with no challenge, he wouldn't
work with me if it would pay the national debt, and he
can't afford to park the car in New York anyway ... No,
this was after he tied me up, but before he started
stumbling around in a stupor ... Yes, yes, I would stay
here, if he said anything about staying, but he hasn't said
anything about staying ... Ellen, I have ... I have ... I have
made a gesture, a three thousand mile bus and taxi from
the airport gesture ... It's his turn ... Yes, I know I have
my own career to think about, but I don't think I'm strong
enough right now. Not only have I not sold a screenplay, I
have also not sold a treatment for a screenplay, or a
proposal for a story idea for a treatment of a screenplay. I
didn't have any idea. So I followed Jimmy Tyrrell's
carefully considered professional advice and wrote about
the alien android who travels in time and meets Atilla the
Hun ... It was called *The Android Who Meets Atilla the
Hun*, what did you expect me to call it, *Moby Dick*! And on
top of everything else, Ellen, Paul found the package of
condoms in my bag ... Of, course, I was embarrassed—
they still had the cellophane on; they were unopened,
virgin condoms. Do you think I should tell him they were
my second pack?... Tenth? Let me see, ten times four each
of three varieties, you know, I think second is fine ... Yes,

I do know tomorrow is another day, Ellen, but because of
the time difference this *is* tomorrow and so far it hasn't
helped. (*Hangs up. Gets up. LID of chest starts to rise.
Instantly remembers SHE has forgotten something. Dials
long distance. Sits on chest. On phone.*) Ellen, I'm sorry ...
No, really, I'm sorry, Ellen ... I know you do. We all do.
We all have other things to do than stay on the phone all
evening. Well, actually, I don't. Personally, I sort of like
living my life on the phone; you don't have to dress, you
can really get intimate, and you probably won't catch
anything ... I know it's not real life, Ellen that's why I like
it ... Yes, I suppose I could watch it. What's on tonight?...
No, I'm sorry? I don't expect you to read me *TV Guide* at
long distance rates ... Oh, yes, let me think, why did I call
again? I remember. Let them know at the temporary
agency that I'm going to be back sooner than expected ...
Well, I need the work, I need the money. I owe Jimmy
Tyrrell for the airline ticket ... Yes, tomorrow. 'Bye.
(*Hangs up. The PHONE rings. POLLY answers. On
phone.*) Yes, hello, Ellen ... Oh, I'm sorry. Who?... Yes, it
is ... Who?... Yes, sure I'll get him.

(*POLLY throws back the lid of the chest. Pauls's hands are
tied behind his back. HE is gagged with the same scarf.
His feet are not tied. Stands in chest. POLLY holds out
phone to him.*)

POLLY. It's Sandra for you, Gummy Bear.

(*PAUL deadpans. POLLY on phone.*)

POLLY. I'm sorry, Gummy Bear can't talk just now,

he's all tied up ... Yes, all right, I'll tell him. 'Bye. (*Hangs up.*) Something's come up and she's going away this weekend. Probably just as well; you don't look too agile, right now.

(*PAUL steps out of chest.*)

POLLY. In fact, you look like a man who's had one martini too many on an empty stomach. (*SHE closes chest.*) I think you may be poised on the brink of a drinking problem. A real drinking problem. If I were staying here, I'd soon fix that. I'd ration you. What do you say to that?

(*PAUL has sat on chest.*)

POLLY. Since you have decided we are not going to work on Miss Charlie, because it doesn't offer you enough challenge, I am going back to California where I can get on with my own life and career. In fact, I was just packing. And I'm taking this. (*Meaning the scarf, which SHE unties and takes off. SHE will toss it in the suitcase. The lemon is jammed between Paul's teeth. HE can not talk.*) I think you're wrong about it all being just formula with no challenge. I think if you work hard enough at those old formulas they can still pay off in surprising ways. But if that's your last word, that's that. Is that your last word? And as for challenging, you want challenging, set yourself free. That'll keep you challenged for about an hour and twenty minutes—I timed it. They you'll be able to go on writing your dreary epitaph for modern marriage. If that's what you want. (*Beat.*) Is that what you want? (*Beat.*) Paul, I want an answer. (*Takes lemon out of his mouth.*)

PAUL. Thank you for not tying my ankles.

POLLY. You weren't going anywhere.

PAUL. Are you going to untie me now?

POLLY. Why should I untie you?

PAUL. Because I don't think I can fix an Alka-Seltzer like this.

POLLY. You didn't untie me. I had to crawl around and find the knife and cut myself free.

PAUL. Well, that was the whole point. You say we can't work together—we just did. And our working together worked.

POLLY. (*Untying him.*) For the last time. I'll get a taxi in the morning and if you sleep late we won't have to talk to one another.

PAUL. (*HE is free.*) Why are you going back?

POLLY. Why? Because I have a very successful screenwriting career to get back to, that's why.

PAUL. Oh.

POLLY. But thank you for asking. The first time I left you didn't even ask.

PAUL. I guess, because I thought you were having a thing with Tommy Fellepelle, I guess.

POLLY. I wasn't. I had a thing for Fellepelle, not with Fellepelle. And it wasn't the money. I just needed to do something on my own. It was always by Paul and Polly Butler. *Miss Charlie's First Case* by Paul and Polly Butler. *Miss Charlie's Second Case* by Paul and Polly Butler. *Charlie's Third* by Paul and Polly Butler. Always Paul and Polly. I wanted it to say by Polly Butler. Screenplay by Polly Butler or something by Polly Butler. Something I did all by myself. Something I could be proud of.

PAUL. Something like *The Android who Met Atilla the*

Hun by Polly Butler. Something like that?

POLLY. *(Indignant.)* That was a private phone call!

PAUL. It's very hard to stick your fingers in your ears with your hands tied behind your back.

POLLY. You heard it all?

PAUL. Every long distance message unit. You're back and right away the phone bill's going through the roof.

POLLY. Okay, so my screenplays are terrible.

PAUL. Like my novel.

POLLY. *(Fast.)* Not that terrible. *(Getting upset.)* Well, what do you want me to say? You want me to just stand here and flat out humiliate myself? You need to hear it? Okay, I went away to do something on my own. I did something on my own and it was a disaster. A complete disaster. There, I've said it. *(Beat.)* I tried. I really tried. They said I didn't have the right feel for science-fiction. They didn't like me. They didn't like my script. They didn't like my android. They hated my android. They said it wasn't appealing enough. They said it wasn't warm enough. They said my android was rude and bossy.

PAUL. *(Comforting.)* Never mind. I'll bet Atilla was perfect.

POLLY. And so, I came back here, here not the Plaza because if you support yourself doing free-lance word processing you can't afford the Plaza. I didn't know that while I was gone you'd found Cassandra and Bombay Gin.

PAUL. Well, the gin is empty. And I found out today that Sandra's throbbing headache is a weightlifter named Ronny. I think she only slept with me because I wrote thrillers and she thought it would be thrilling. Thank God, I don't write comedy.

POLLY. It's rough out there, Paul.

PAUL. You mean California?

POLLY. No, I mean the other side of the door. It's rough out there, and I've got the bruises to prove it. I know I'm not perfect but I'm not that terrible person in your novel. I mean, I did not leave you to starve or drive you to drink.

PAUL. Oh yes, you did. Yes, you did. *(Means it.)* When you weren't here, you drove me to drink.

POLLY. Oh.

PAUL. *(Pause. As if she had just arrived.)* Hello, Polly. Good to see you. How've you been?

POLLY. Fine. *(Beat.)* How are you? How's everyone— friends, drinking buddies, everyone?

PAUL. Fine. *(Beat.)* Everyone's fine. The ... the buddies in the bar downstairs have dwindled down to a precious few. Know what I mean?

POLLY. I know what you mean. Peggy and Muffy have kids and Ellen has group therapy.

PAUL. I know what you mean.

POLLY. I have a reservation on TWA.

PAUL. I know. *(Beat.)* Listen, there is something else I wanted to ...

(KNOCK, KNOCK very loud at the front door.
Beat. BOTH look at front door. Beat. BOTH look at each other.)

POLLY. What's that?
PAUL. Bad timing.
POLLY. There's someone at the door.
PAUL. There can't be.

(KNOCK, KNOCK. BOTH look at front door.
Then back at each other.)

POLLY. There is. Are you expecting anyone?

PAUL. No. Are you?

POLLY. No. It's pretty late.

PAUL. And you're here.

POLLY. And you're here. Who could it be?

PAUL. *(Crossing.)* Well, there's one way to find out, I guess.

POLLY. Probably no one.

PAUL. You're probably right. *(Opens door.)*

POLLY. Who is it?

PAUL. No one.

POLLY. That's what I thought.

PAUL. There's no one in sight.

POLLY. It might have been some kids.

PAUL. That's very strange. Wait a minute. *(Stoops.)* There's something here—a package. *(Brings into the room, closing door, a package which was on the floor just outside the front door.)* Not the mailman. No stamp. By hand—obviously.

POLLY. Who's it for?

PAUL. Us. Both of us. Paul and Polly Butler.

POLLY. You're always first—Paul and Polly Butler. Paul and Polly. The man is always first. It's not fair. They should do it alphabetically.

PAUL. I'd still be first.

POLLY. Oh. Well, what is it? Open it.

PAUL. *(Examining package.)* There's nothing on it. Our names, that's all. *(Puts it down.)*

POLLY. Are you going to open it or not?

PAUL. (*Sharply.*) Did you send this?

POLLY. No, I didn't send it. (*Beat.*) Did you?

PAUL. No, be quiet.

POLLY. Why?

PAUL. I want to hear if it's ticking.

POLLY. You want to hear if it's what?

PAUL. Ticking. You know ticking: tick-tock, tick-tock.

POLLY. Why would anyone send us a clock?

PAUL. Because it was wired to dynamite. As in tick-tock boom-boom.

POLLY. You're just trying to frighten me. You sent it and you're trying to frighten me.

PAUL. I didn't send it.

POLLY. Well, is it?

PAUL. What?

POLLY. (*Snaps.*) Ticking?

PAUL. (*Puts his hear to package.*) No. Maybe we should put it in a bucket of water?

POLLY. Good idea. Unless, it's alive. (*HE looks at her.*) Well, someone might have sent us some baby chicks.

PAUL. Who in the name of God would send us baby chicks?

POLLY. Well, I don't know. Listen and see if it's cheeping.

PAUL. It's not cheeping.

POLLY. You haven't listened.

PAUL. I listened for ticking, I'd have noticed cheeping.

POLLY. Or a kitten. Listen for meowing. Or hissing. Please tell me, it isn't hissing. Or rattling?

(*PAUL has ripped the brown paper open. It contains a very, very large, very, very expensive box of chocolates.)*

PAUL. Wow! Look at that. Will you look at that.

POLLY. I'm looking, Paul, I'm looking.

PAUL. Chocolates. Five pounds. A five pound box of the world's most expensive chocolate.

POLLY. Finally, chocolates in a size that fits. Nobody likes us this much. (*Reverently.*) Paul. Take the lid off. (*HE does so.*) Take out the tissue. (*HE does so.*) Take out that other thing. (*HE does so.*) There they are.

PAUL. Naked.

POLLY. I should die now; I'm in a state of grace.

PAUL. Suddenly I don't want to have sex anymore. Sex is a form of sharing. And I don't want to share.

POLLY. Who's it from?

PAUL. I dunno. There's no card. I dunno.

POLLY. It doesn't matter; they're going to heaven whoever they are. (*Pointing.*) You see that round, dark chocolate one with the little squiggle on top?

PAUL. Yes.

POLLY. It's a raspberry buttercream.

PAUL. (*Jealously.*) And I suppose you want it?

POLLY. Five pounds, Paul, five pounds. This box has lots of raspberry buttercreams. (*HE hands her the chocolate.*) Thank you. I can go back to California a happy woman. (*Her hand on the way to her mouth.*) I think, I have the same thing for chocolates you have for martinis. (*Her hand freezes. Pause.*) You sent those, didn't you?

PAUL. No.

POLLY. You put these outside the door?

PAUL. No.

POLLY. You did. You did. Admit it.

PAUL. I was here with you the whole time. You saw me. I never left the apartment.

POLLY. You paid someone to deliver them. I remember that first martini, Paul. I'm not falling for that twice in a row. I'm going to bite into this raspberry buttercream and it's going to be full of hot Chinese mustard and you're going to yell gotcha! You must think I was born yesterday. (*Puts chocolate down.*)

PAUL. I did not send them.

POLLY. I don't believe you.

PAUL. I did not send them. I promise you, I did not send them. I'll prove it. I'll eat one.

POLLY. Oh, sure. You know which ones you tampered with. You'll get a Rum Truffle. And then I'll get something with little bits of pimento in it.

PAUL. Okay. All right. You choose it. You choose it, and I'll eat it.

POLLY. Okay. Let me see. Let me see. This one. Eat that. (*Hands him chocolate. As SHE does.*)

PAUL. You gotta admit, the martini was great. I knew you would switch glasses, I knew it. A double bluff. (*Freezes. Beat.*) Well done, Polly, well done. I nearly fell for it. (*As HE puts it down.*) What's in there, anchovy paste?

POLLY. What do you mean?

PAUL. You sent them, didn't you? All that Chinese mustard stuff was just a set up.

POLLY. No, I didn't send them, you did. You sent them.

PAUL. I did not send them, I swear it on my mother's grave!

POLLY. Your mother's still alive!

PAUL. Yeah, well, she's got a plot already!

(Pause.)

POLLY. I've never been so unhappy in my life. There's nothing I wouldn't do for that box of chocolates. For all those truffles and buttercreams I'd do the trip over—plane, bus, taxi, everything. The whole public transportation mess. But they're poisoned.

PAUL. *(Absently.)* I didn't send them.

POLLY. I'm going to gamble. Nobody could tamper with them all; there's too many.

PAUL. *(Thinking aloud.)* You know, if life had a plot like a mystery story there'd be clues, wouldn't there? And somewhere along the way the great detective, or even Miss Charlie, would know the solution and say something cryptic.

POLLY. I won't take the raspberry buttercream. That's my favorite. It's probably lethal.

PAUL. Something cryptic like ... public transportation. Oh, my God, we haven't been paying attention. That's the clue!

POLLY. Orange. Orange buttercream is my second favorite. *(Poised to eat.)*

PAUL. *(Quietly urgent.)* Don't eat that.

POLLY. I'm not on a diet.

PAUL. Don't eat that.

POLLY. Why not?

PAUL. Because real life may have a plot.

CURTAIN

Scene 6

*The next morning. PAUL is asleep, in the sleeping bag
wearing pajamas. The chocolates with the box lid off
are on the chest. Polly's suitcase open, DR chair.
POLLY, dressed, enters from the bathroom carrying a
toilet kit, crosses to the suitcase and puts it in. Looks
around. Closes suitcase. Gets handbag. Is ready.*

POLLY. (*SHE wouldn't mind if Paul woke.*) Okay. I'm
set. Is there anything I've forgotten? Guess not. (*To Paul
though SHE knows he is asleep.*) Well, that's it, all packed
and ready to go back to Hollywood land of the androids.
I'll send you a postcard—Having a wonderful time, wish
you were here ... wish I were ... Well, never mind, doesn't
matter, we'll both be okay, I guess, though you, of course,
live in chaos and buy gallons of gin. I, on the other hand,
do extremely well because I'm busy and efficient and neat
and tidy and organized, except that I find I make a lot of
long distance phone calls in the middle of the night. You
want to know something, even if I had had a lot of money,
I wouldn't have stayed at the Plaza, because the Plaza
wasn't where I wanted to be. Here is where I wanted to be.
In an empty rent-stabilized studio on the floor in a sleeping
bag. I know you said it was uncomfortable ... but Paul you
were my comfort then. (*Checks watch.*) Is there anything I
want? Anything at all? (*Beat.*) I guess, I don't want
anything.

(*Exits front door—SLAMMING door. PAUL reacts to slam*

*without waking. Pause. Sound of KEY in door. POLLY
enters, puts case and bag down right inside door.)*

POLLY. Yes, by God, there is something I want.
(*Crossing to chocolates.*) A raspberry buttercream. Five
pounds of chocolates and due to your paranoia, I haven't
had a single one. (*Reaches into chocolate box. Freezes.
Beat. Suddenly jumps onto the foot of the bed, screaming.*)
Paul! Paul! Paul!

PAUL. (*Sits up, completely disoriented.*) What! What!
What!

POLLY. Wake up! Wake up!

PAUL. I'm awake! I'm awake!

POLLY. There's a mouse! There's a mouse!

PAUL. (*Getting up in sleeping bag.*) Where! Where!

POLLY. (*Pointing to chocolates.*) It's right there! It's
right there!

PAUL. Stop saying it twice! Stop saying in twice! Get a
grip on yourself.

(SHE clutches him. HE is struggling out of sleeping bag.)

PAUL. That's not yourself. That's me.

POLLY. There's a mouse right there.

PAUL. I told you I had mice.

(BOTH looking down on chocolates and mouse.)

POLLY. What are we going to do?

PAUL. Well, now that we're up it'll go away.

POLLY. Well, it's not going. See.

PAUL. (*Stooped. Peering at it.*) No. And I don't think

it's going to go as long as it has all four of those tiny little feet up in the air like that.

POLLY. What do you mean?

PAUL. (*Stepping off bed.*) It's dead. Dead as a doornail. I wonder what killed it?

POLLY. Maybe it saw all those chocolates and died of joy. (*SHE will get down.*)

PAUL. I don't think so. It's eaten part of one.

POLLY. Oh, let me see, let me see. That's marzipan I always leave marzipan 'till last.

PAUL. It ate about two-thirds.

POLLY. Too much rich food and then a tiny heart attack.

PAUL. (*Picking up mouse by the tail. POLLY steps back.*) These chocolates are poisoned.

POLLY. I knew you sent them.

PAUL. Not poisoned cute. Poisoned real. This mouse was murdered.

POLLY. Those are really poisoned.

PAUL. This is really murder.

POLLY. Paul, this is real life. What do we do? What do we do?

PAUL. We're Miss Charlie. We solve it. (*Considers.*) Poisoned and sent by hand, with no note, to Paul and Polly Butler.

POLLY. (*Pause.*) What does that mean?

PAUL. It means, somebody tried to kill us. We're supposed to be dead.

POLLY. For real?

PAUL. For real. (*Working it out.*) Okay, okay. Let me think. Whatta we do? We assemble all the suspects. We review the case. What do we know? Chocolates are your

favorite weapon. You said so yourself, remember.
Everyone knew that. A lot of people knew that we
rehearsed our murders. A smaller group, a much smaller
group, knew you were coming to New York. Who?

POLLY. Well, Jimmy Tyrrell and Ellen. That's it. I
think that's it.

PAUL. And I told Sandra.

POLLY. (*Indignant.*) Well, it was probably Sandra!

PAUL. No, they wanted us *both* dead. I may have told
the Fellepelles, but they're away. Someone may have seen
you in the building—Hayakawa and Charlotte Brown,
remember.

POLLY. It was Charlotte Brown! She's going to marry
him then she'll be Charlotte Hayakawa aka Miss Charlie.
She wanted to kill Miss Charlie.

PAUL. You got it backwards. We were the intended
victims not Miss Charlie. Miss Charlie recently became
very valuable. Why aren't you writing her yourself?

POLLY. 'Cos you own half the copyright.

PAUL. Unless, until ... public transportation.
Remember you said, if we were both hit by a bus, a public
bus, the copyright went to ...

POLLY. Jimmy Tyrrell. Our agent.

PAUL. Jimmy Tyrrell—who paid for your ticket to get
us together. The *most likely* suspect!

POLLY. I don't believe it. I *do* believe it.

PAUL. That sleazy, greedy son-of-a-bitch!

POLLY. Wait 'till I land in L.A. Am I going to give
him a piece of my mind.

PAUL. Are you crazy? You're not going anywhere!
The man has tried to kill you. You're staying here.
(*Pause.*) I want you to stay. I'm intelligent, I'm clever, I'm

talented, I'm here, I'm alone, I'm nothing.

POLLY. *(Pause. SHE has heard him.)* Well, we'll both be nothing if he tries again, Paul. Whatta we do? Whatta we do?

PAUL. *(Patiently.)* We change the will. *(Enjoying it.)* The man's an idiot. I mean, we may not be much apart, but together we're Miss Charlie. And Miss Charlie loves a challenge. Hot damn, think of the publicity.

POLLY. Now what?

PAUL. Now? Well, we've solved the case. So ... now, I guess you want the aspirin back in the bathroom.

POLLY. But, Paul, we have nothing in common.

PAUL. Sure, we do. Jigsaw puzzles. We both like jigsaw puzzles. I like spreading them out and doing them and you like putting them back in the box before I'm finished. It's a perfect match.

POLLY. We fight all the time.

PAUL. That wasn't fighting. That was foreplay. *(Beat.)* Listen, I know the sleeping bag was romantic, but the floor is hard and we bought furniture since then and we're older now and I have my bad back and I'm not as agile as I was and can we use the bed, please?

POLLY. Gotcha.

CURTAIN

PROPERTY LIST

Scene 1
Suitcase, briefcase, handbag (Polly)
Paper bag and dagger with disappearing blade (Polly)
Compact (Polly)
Paper bag and bottle of gin (Paul)
Latex gloves (Polly)
Two martinis (Paul)
Lemon peel (Paul)

Scene 2
Stocking or pantyhose (Polly)
Dirty laundry in chest (Set)
Pantyhose prearranged as mask in chest (Set)
Large axe in chest (Set)
Black bra (Set)
Pistol in dirty clothes (Set)
Typescript, unbound (Set)
Clean shirts with cardboard (Set)
Toilet kit (Paul)
Magic marker (Set)

Scene 3
Blanket and pillow (Set)
Coffee mug (Paul)
Shotgun (Set) Shotgun shell (Set); Emptying the shell
should be cheated so it is fast.
String (Set)
Glass of water (Paul)

Scene 4
Handbag (Polly) containing:
    Hair brush
    Pill bottle
    Billfold
    Keys
    Compact
    Silk scarf
    Address book
    Hairspray
    Flashlight
    Airline ticket
    Candy bar
    Handkerchief
    Packet of condoms
    Clothesline
Kitchen knife (Paul)
Pitcher of martinis, two glasses (Paul)
Checklist (Set)
Lemon (Paul)
Cigar, matches (Set)

Scene 5
Box of chocolates in wrapping paper (Set)

Scene 6
Toilet kit (Polly)
Sleeping bag (Set)
"Dead mouse" (Set)

NOTES

Please note that the costume and property changes between scenes are minimal and can be done very quickly.

Polly wears the same clothes in scenes one and two and can put a bathrobe over them for scene three. Paul wears the same clothes throughout Act I, except for a shirt changed during the action.

In Act II Polly wears the same clothes (with knee pads under the slacks) throughout with a coat or jacket added for Scene 6. Paul wears the same thing for Scenes 4 and 5 and changes into "pajamas" for Scene 6, but a T-shirt and maybe sweat pants might be worn under his other clothes.

During intermission, the set is tidied and the furniture positions adjusted slightly as described in the stage directions.

NOTE that the directions in Scene 3 state that Paul has backed well away from Polly before she fires the gun. Care should be taken even with blanks. In some venues, with older audiences, it may be advisable for the program to state in small print: "There are gunshots in Scene 3." This will not undercut the play.

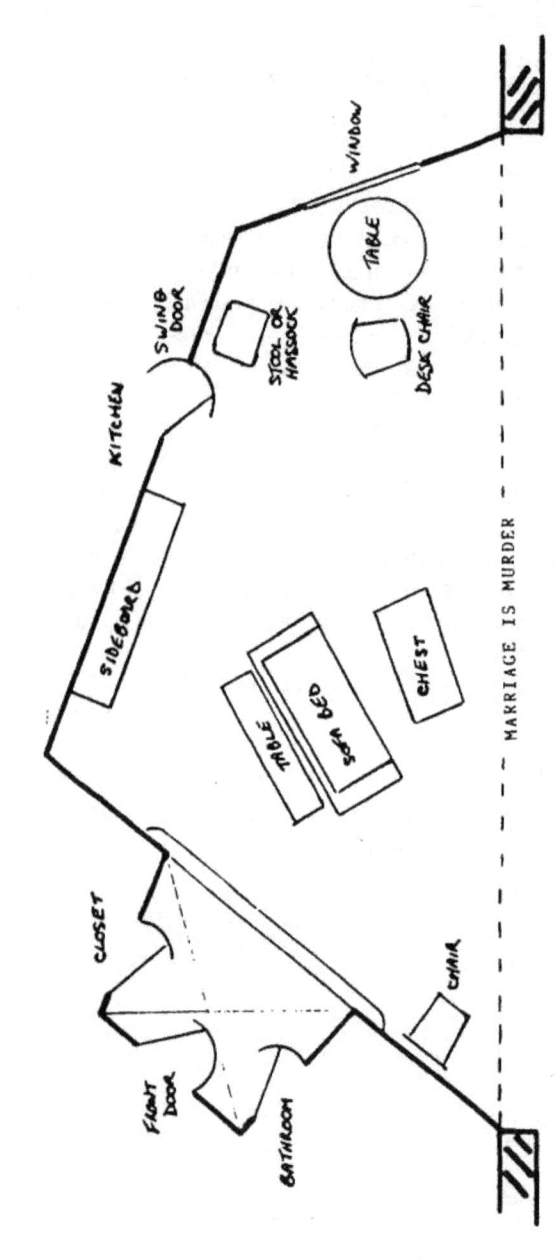

KITCHEN

SWING DOOR

STOOL OR HASSOCK

TABLE

WINDOW

DESK CHAIR

SIDEBOARD

TABLE

SOFA BED

CHEST

CLOSET

FRONT DOOR

BATHROOM

CHAIR

-- MARRIAGE IS MURDER --

www.ingramcontent.com/pod-product-compliance
Lightning Source LLC
Chambersburg PA
CBHW071929130726
47909CB00014B/2837